Tiny the Prickly Plant

story by Elsie Nelley

lustrations by
enny Mountstephen

Tiny Owl saw a hole up in a prickly plant.

"This will be a good nest for my eggs," she said.

4

Tiny Owl sat down
inside the hole.

"My eggs will be safe
in here," she said.

Tiny Owl saw a big cat coming by.

The big cat looked up.
"I like to eat owls," he said.
"Only I can't get this owl.
The plant is too prickly."

A brown snake came by.

He saw Tiny Owl
inside the hole.

"I like to eat bird eggs,"
he said.
"Only I can't climb up
prickly plants."

A hungry fox saw Tiny Owl looking down at him.

"Have you got some eggs in your nest?" he said.

"Yes," said Tiny Owl.

"Only you can't get up here," said Tiny Owl.

"No," said the fox. "You are too clever for me."

So away he went.

"I am clever," said Tiny Owl.
"This hole is a **good** nest.
The big cat,
the brown snake,
and the hungry fox
can't get up here."

So Tiny Owl went to sleep.